The
Big Box

by Grace DiGange
illustrated by Wallace Keller

 HOUGHTON MIFFLIN   BOSTON

The fox can see the big box!

The fox can fit in the big box.

Here is a pig.
The pig can fit in the big box, too.

One, two, three, four, five!
The animals jump in the big box!

The ox can not fit in the big box now.

The animals are NOT in the big box.

The fox and the pig and one, two, three, four, five do not fit. Now the ox can fit in the big box.